CHEETAHS

MAGGIE PEARSON

Donnabella

illustrated by
Amelia Rosato

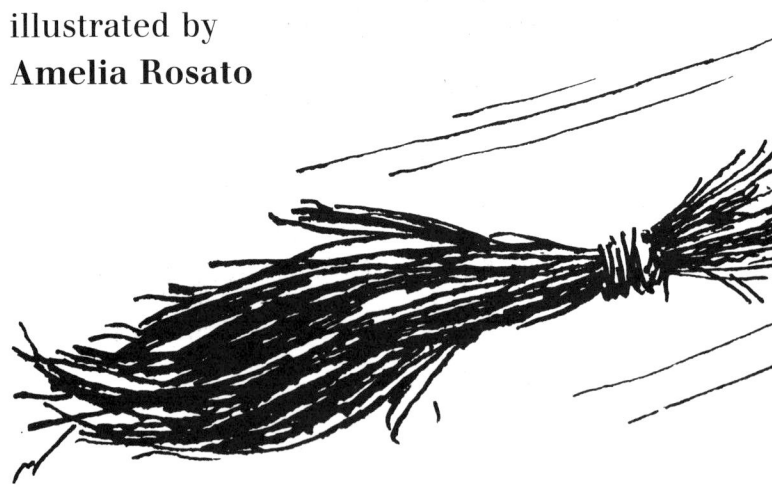

HODDER AND STOUGHTON
London   Sydney   Auckland   Toronto

British Library Cataloguing in Publication Data

Pearson, Maggie
   Donnabella.
   I. Title   II. Rosato, Amelia   III. Series
   823'.914 [J]

   ISBN 0-340-42936-4

Published by Hodder and Stoughton Children's Books,
a division of Hodder and Stoughton Ltd,
Mill Road, Dunton Green, Sevenoaks, Kent TN13 2YJ

Photoset by Litho Link Ltd, Welshpool, Powys

Printed in Great Britain by St Edmundsbury Press Ltd,
Bury St Edmunds, Suffolk

Contents

Miss Plint, Familiar

Chapter 1

Resp[ec]table
witch
familiar

No exp[...]
As tr[...]

Live [...]

NO CATS

RESPECTABLE WITCH SEEKS FAMILIAR
NO EXPERIENCE NEEDED
AS TRAINING GIVEN
LIVE IN

Donnabella pinned the notice to her front gate and read it through again. She frowned, licked her pencil, and added: NO CATS.

Cats, thought Donnabella, as she stumped back indoors, were nasty creatures. The sort of nasty creatures who sharpen their claws on your broomstick, so that it lets you down with a bump over Bramble Wood.

She kicked the two halves of the broomstick into a corner and ate her tea standing up, because the place she sat on still felt sore. She pondered about the best sort of familiar to choose. It must be quite tall, so that it could reach things down from the top shelf while she was mixing spells. That ruled out frogs – besides, they always had wet feet.

It must be clever, but not too clever. Owls were too clever by half.

If Donnabella had pondered all night, she would never have thought of what actually turned up.

There was quite a queue outside the gate
next morning. A dog, three bats, a little old
lady, and two small boys who ran off as
soon as Donnabella gave them a look.

'No cats?' asked the dog, pointing to the
notice.

'Positively no cats,' said Donnabella.

'Spoilsport,' snapped the dog, and trotted
off down the road.

By this time the three bats had gone to
sleep, hanging in a row like raindrops from
the top bar of the gate. So that left –

'Agatha Plint, ma'am,' said the little old
lady, with a little bob. 'I should like to apply

for the position as advertised.' She stood
with her toes turned out, clutching her
handbag in both hands.

'But you're a person,' said Donnabella.

Miss Plint read the notice through
carefully. 'It doesn't say NO PERSONS, as
far as I can see. Just NO CATS.'

'That's because they don't usually apply
for the job,' said Donnabella. 'Do you know
what a familiar is?'

'Well, I suppose it's some sort of assistant
witch, isn't it? Someone to pass you things
when you're mixing spells, and tidy up
afterwards. I can also do cookery and
needlework, and gardening, and a little
light housework, and if there's anything
else – ' she pointed to the notice, ' – it does
say TRAINING GIVEN.'

The more Donnabella thought about the idea, the more she liked it – especially the bit about tidying up.

'I expect you could do with some help about the house,' added Miss Plint, 'with the Coven meeting here tonight.' She pointed to a squiggly mark chalked on the gatepost. 'Sign-reading,' she explained. 'I picked it up in the Girl Guides.'

Donnabella made up her mind. 'All right,' she said. 'Can you start at once?'

Miss Plint blinked. She supposed she could. She blinked again and almost changed her mind when Donnabella led the way indoors.

Witches are never the tidiest of people, and Donnabella was not the tidiest of witches. A thick film of evil-smelling dust hung over everything. Great black cobwebs dangled from the beams. The grime on the windows was so thick that not a chink of sunlight managed to struggle through. The only light came from the fire that smoked glumly on the hearth.

'It's very – unusual,' said Miss Plint politely.

'Glad you like it,' said Donnabella. 'Make
yourself at home. I'm off to buy a new
broom.' She slammed the door behind her
and the dust swirled and rose and fell,
settling itself into new patterns on the
furniture.

A new broom, thought Miss Plint. That's
just what this place needs. A new broom to
sweep it clean. Well, I suppose that's me.
She set to work with a will.

Tidying Up
Chapter 2

It really wasn't turning out to be such a bad day, thought Donnabella, as she stepped out towards the town. She'd found herself some free help around the house, and tonight the Annual General Meeting of the local Coven was to be held there.

That had been a close thing: Grimalda had been very keen to offer her home, but, as Donnabella pointed out, if they were going to meet in a draughty old castle, they might as well hold the meeting in the open air and have done with it. So, with a casting vote from the chairperson, Vampira, who had caught a nasty chill last time she left her nice warm coffin for an evening at Grimalda's, Donnabella had carried the day.

As for having to buy a new broom – she had been meaning to treat herself to one for a long time.

There in the garden shop they seemed to have the very thing. The notice in the window said clearly:
GENUINE WITCHES BROOMS
NO HOME SHOULD BE WITHOUT ONE
IDEAL FOR SHORT TRIPS
The manager had put it up as a joke,

thinking it would bring in more customers,
but he began to wish he hadn't as
Donnabella stood outside the shop trying
to get her new broom to start. She coaxed
it. She threatened it. She threw it on the
ground and jumped on it, while a small but
interested crowd gathered to see whether
she really would turn the manager into a
frog, as she kept threatening to do.

In the end, he offered to give her her
money back – and let her keep the broom
as well.

'What on earth,' snapped Donnabella,
'would I do with a broom that can't fly?'

But she took it, just the same. The odd spell or two might put it in working order. 'Besides, I'm not going to be beaten by an overgrown heap of firewood,' she hissed to the broom, as she tucked it under her arm and set out for home. She did not know what had been going on there while she had been away.

A cat, or an owl, or any ordinary familiar, when told to make itself at home, would have snuggled down beside the fire and gone to sleep. But Miss Plint was no ordinary familiar. She had gone through the house like a breath of fresh air (which was something it badly needed), tidying and dusting and polishing, so that when she came in poor Donnabella hardly recognised her own home.

'Aaaargh!' she screamed. 'What have you done to my lovely house?'

'I thought I'd make a start,' beamed Miss Plint. 'Excuse me.' She bustled outside to shake her duster.

Donnabella stared round her. All her lovely cobwebs! The dust she'd been collecting for years! Gone! All gone. Worse still, what were her friends going to think? The disgrace of it! She would never live it down.

'What am I going to do?' moaned Donnabella.

'It's not as bad as all that,' beamed Miss Plint, bustling back in. 'We've plenty of time to finish getting things straight before your friends arrive. Now, if you could just sniff these jars and tell me what's in them, I'll put some sticky labels on and line them up in alphabetical order.'

'Don't open that jar!' screamed Donnabella, diving forward – too late!

Off came the lid, clouds of dust billowed upwards and left the two of them too busy coughing and spluttering to speak. Slowly

the dust turned into a cloud of rainbow-coloured mist. Miss Plint stopped coughing and looked about her. 'What's happened?' she asked in a small voice. 'Where's the furniture?'

'What happened,' said Donnabella, 'is that you opened a jar of the very best vanishing powder I ever made, and spilt several times the normal dose, so that we've both vanished into thin air. I've a very good mind to leave you here, you – you mortal!'

She strode away into the mist, leaving Miss Plint to follow as best she could. 'Please wait,' she panted. 'I'm getting terribly out of breath!'

'What do you expect?' snapped Donnabella. 'It *is* thin air!'

Miss Plint plunged after her just before she vanished into the mist. She had an uneasy feeling they were not alone. Out of the corner of her eye she could see strange

shapes moving about. Then one jumped
straight across the path and she saw it was
a rabbit. Most of them were; though there
were doves as well, and once a whole shoal
of goldfish swam past, not seeming to mind
at all that there was no water.

They walked for a long time, until at last
Donnabella pointed out a gleam of light.
As they came closer, they saw it was a
young lady in a bathing costume covered
with sequins, and beside her – Miss Plint
gave a sigh of relief – was a door.

'Excuse me,' said Donnabella, elbowing
the young lady to one side. The two elderly
ladies stepped through the door and were
greeted with loud applause from the theatre
audience, who had quite clearly seen one

young lady step into the magician's cabinet.

They made their escape while the magician was still wondering where his assistant could have got to.

Donnabella hadn't judged her landfall too badly, but it was still a long walk home.

Two very footsore ladies made their way up Donnabella's garden path with only ten minutes to spare before the Coven meeting. The room looked even worse than Donnabella remembered; all shiny and clean. One lonely spider was spinning a web high up on a beam, but without much enthusiasm.

Donnabella said nothing, but stumped off upstairs to put a few extra tangles in her hair before the others arrived.

The Coven
Chapter 3

M iss Plint looked glumly round. She felt she wasn't making a great success as a familiar.

There was already another spider's web up there. With the broom she might just be able to reach it . . .

And then things began to happen. Perhaps the broom was naturally mischievous; perhaps it hadn't liked Donnabella calling it an overgrown heap of firewood; but once it swung into action, there was no stopping it.

The terrified spider swung from beam to beam, spinning for dear life, with the broom always close behind it. When the spider finally managed to hide in a crack in the ceiling, the broom started on the floor, producing clouds of dust from nowhere. It swung past the fireplace and clouds of smoke billowed into the room. Miss Plint was dragged along behind it, willy-nilly, round and round, over and under, until she didn't know whether she was on her head or her heels.

At last her cries brought Donnabella – and that was when the fun really started. Donnabella threw spell after spell at the

runaway broom. Most of them it dodged
easily and they splashed into the wall,
making oddly shaped stains. Some rolled
harmlessly into corners. Then the broom
gained confidence and began batting them
back and sent Donnabella and Miss Plint
running for cover. It was beginning to look
like a dangerous sort of cricket, with the
broom on the winning side, when a voice
from the doorway exclaimed:

'Why, Donnabella, what a surprise!
You've been redecorating.'

'Isn't it beautiful!' cried another.
'So modern!'

The broom stopped. It couldn't believe
its bristles.

Witch after witch moved about the room,
exclaiming at the cobwebs, the dust and the
marks on the wall.

'So artistic!' they said.

'So unusual!'

'It must have taken weeks of work!'

'My! Something smells good!'

The broom gave up and slunk away into
a corner to sulk.

Needless to say, the evening was a great

success and in the kitchen while they were
getting tea, Donnabella said to Miss Plint,
'You know, you might not turn out to be
such a bad familiar after all.'

Credit where credit's due, thought
Donnabella: if Miss Plint hadn't tidied up,
and opened the jar that made them vanish,
and picked up the broom that got out of
control . . . Grimalda, thought Donnabella
happily, was quite green with envy.

Grimalda, if Donnabella had but known
it, was already plotting mischief.

'A familiar!' she murmured to Miss Plint.
'My dear, you're wasted as a familiar.
It's Donnabella, of course. Keeping you
back, the mean thing! Haven't you ever
thought of becoming a witch yourself!'

'A witch?' gasped Miss Plint. 'Me?'

'I'll lend you some books. Try a little spell or two. You'll find you have a natural talent, mark my words.'

'Oh!' said Miss Plint. 'Have I really?'

'You could be a full member of the Coven by Hallowe'en, if I'm any judge. Not a word to Donnabella, though. Let's surprise her.'

Donnabella, of course, would have warned Miss Plint that Grimalda was not to be trusted. Grimalda was the sort that gets witches a bad name. The sort that liked to make mischief for mischief's sake. But poor Miss Plint thought Grimalda the nicest witch she'd met so far.

'Oh, one other thing, my dear,' said Grimalda. 'You must insist on having your own broomstick. That funny little thing of Donnabella's was never meant to carry two. You could take a nasty tumble over Bramble Wood.'

Off she went in a cloud of sparks, on her new super-broom, and riding behind her, on a velvet cushion, a cat with sharpened claws that would have looked very familiar to Donnabella.

Oh! thought Miss Plint. If only I could learn to fly like that. Riding a broomstick, she soon found out, is not nearly as easy as it looks.

'Why does it have to be a broomstick anyway?' she protested a few days later, after coming in to land hanging upside down, as if from a trapeze. 'Why can't we use something that's meant to be sat on?'

'Oh, yes,' sniffed Donnabella. 'I can just imagine it. Look! Up in the sky! Is it a bird? Is it a plane? Is it Superman? No! It's a witch on a bicycle. It would sound ridiculous.'

'I don't think it likes me,' said Miss Plint.

'Why should it? You've just said *you* don't like *it.*'

Miss Plint patted the broomstick. 'Nice broomstick,' she said. The broomstick gave a jerk. 'You see?' she said.

'Look,' said Donnabella, 'either you learn to fly solo, or you ride pillion behind me. Which is it to be?'

Miss Plint, remembering Grimalda's warning about nasty tumbles from overloaded broomsticks, got back on, wishing she at least had a seat-belt.

'Right!' said Donnabella. 'Now, think upwards. Not too far! You're not going to the moon. Steady. Now. Once round Hemlock Hill and mind how you go over Bramble Wood. And whatever you do, don't look down!'

Miss Plint immediately looked down and wished she hadn't. She shut her eyes tightly and clung to the broomstick with both hands as it pranced away towards Hemlock Hill. It made Donnabella feel quite seasick watching her. So she closed her eyes, leaned back and went to sleep.

The Shrinking Spacemen
Chapter 4

So it was that there was no one at all to see the flying saucer's historic landing a few minutes later – which was just as well, as it was a very bad one.

It appeared from nowhere, out of a clear blue sky, missed the roof of the cottage by no more than a centimetre, skidded sideways and thudded to rest in the middle of Donnabella's hemlock patch, looking like an overgrown mushroom.

'That landing,' said Captain Pfft, picking himself up off the floor, 'was a disgrace to Starfleet.'

'Well, how was I to know that green stuff wasn't solid,' muttered Lieutenant Kchw. 'Records never give us enough information about these primitive planets.'

'Let's hope the natives don't judge us by first impressions.'

'It's all right,' said the Lieutenant. 'There aren't any.'

'No cheering crowds?'

'Not that I noticed.'

'No mass panic?'

The Lieutenant shook his head.

'No one at all?'

'Well, just one. But it seems to be asleep.'

They peered out of the porthole at Donnabella hovering peacefully just above ground level. It had taken a bit of practice, but she found it a lot easier than putting up a deckchair.

'Fascinating,' murmured Lieutenant Kchw. 'They can levitate. I must tell Records.'

'Never mind Records,' snapped Captain Pfft. 'What do we do now? I can't deliver my "People of Earth" speech to an audience of one.'

'Then may I suggest Plan B, Captain?'

The Captain nodded: 'Plan B it is. And do smarten yourself up, Kchw.'

The Lieutenant straightened his ears until they stood up in sharp points before following his Captain down the ramp for their first meeting with a typical human.

The Captain cleared his throat, then turned to the Lieutenant. 'I feel such an idiot,' he said. 'You do it.'

'You are the Captain,' said Kchw. 'But if you feel strongly about it – ' He stepped forward and said loudly, 'Take me to your leader!'

Donnabella opened one eye. 'Pardon?' she said.

Pfft elbowed his Lieutenant aside. 'I am Captain Pfft of Starfleet Command. Our five year mission is to seek out new life . . .'

'And new civilisations,' put in Lieutenant Kchw.

'. . . To boldly go where no man has gone before,' they chorused.

Donnabella opened both eyes and tilted herself into a sitting position. Although both spacemen were only a metre or so high, and bright green, with red beards and enormous pointed ears, she didn't scream or faint or do any of the things they had been warned might happen. She looked straight past them at the spaceship.

'Is that thing yours?' she demanded.

This was more like it, thought the Captain. Naturally, she was impressed by the ship.

'We come from sky in big grey bird,' he said, very slowly and clearly.

'Then kindly get big grey bird off my prize hemlock,' said Donnabella, 'before I turn you both into frogs.'

'Can she do that?' hissed the Captain.

Kchw shook his head. 'Never in a million years,' he said; and added smugly, 'Even we can't do that.'

Meanwhile, Donnabella, reflecting that two frogs wouldn't be much good at moving anything, decided instead to shrink the ship to a manageable size. Before their eyes, the pride of Starfleet shrank to a puny fifty centimetres high.

'I suppose she can't do that either,' snarled the Captain. He was beginning to feel that things were not going according to plan, but it was hard to see where he had gone wrong.

He was not to know that the hemlock was Donnabella's pride and joy. For months she had tended it, weeded it and watered it and had been sure of winning first prize at the flower show that year – until these two hooligans had crept up on it while her back was turned and flattened it with their oversized mushroom.

Captain Pfft folded his arms. 'Very clever,' he said. 'We can't move it now – even if we wanted to – all the controls are inside.'

Donnabella solved that problem very quickly. In a moment both little green men found themselves knee-high to a foxglove.

'Now you can move it,' said Donnabella. 'Can't you?'

'I can,' said the Captain. 'But I won't.' He could be every bit as stubborn as Donnabella. 'It stays right where it is. And so do we until you return us all to our proper size.'

'Do you think it's wise to anger it, sir?' asked Lieutenant Kchw.

It was not wise.

'Please yourselves,' said Donnabella. 'Stay right where you are then.' She closed her eyes and tilted backwards to resume her nap.

Captain Pfft tried to take a step towards her, but his legs would not move. Nor would his arms, his hands, or his head. When Donnabella said, Stay right where you are, that was where you stayed.

Captain Pfft made one last effort to move his legs, and fell flat on his face.

Bad Vibrations
Chapter 5

It was at this point that Miss Plint arrived back on the scene, after a rather bumpy ride round Hemlock Hill.

'Coo-ee,' she cried. 'How do I land?'

'Think downwards,' shouted Donnabella. 'Not straight down!' She dived out of the way just in time as Miss Plint and the broomstick arrived more or less together in a heap on the grass.

Fascinating, mused Lieutenant Kchw. Heavier-than-air flight on an object without wings or motor. Wait till I tell Records! It was nothing to what Captain Pfft was going to tell Records if he ever got back!

'Oh dear,' sighed Miss Plint, picking herself up. 'I was doing so well too. It really is quite fun, once you get the hang of it. You can see for miles. Oh, garden gnomes! Aren't they sweet? Complete with their own dear little mushroom house. Look, it's got real little doors and little windows. You can even see furniture inside. Wherever did they come from?'

'I don't know,' snapped Donnabella. 'But I wish they'd go away.' She had lost interest in the visitors and was busy trying

to coax the hemlock to stand upright again.

Miss Plint picked up the gnomes under one arm and the mushroom under the other and took them round the front of the cottage, out of Donnabella's way. There she met Witch Hazel, who was collecting for the Coven jumble sale that afternoon.

'Did Donnabella put those out for me?' asked Witch Hazel.

'Well,' said Miss Plint, 'she doesn't seem to want them any more, so I suppose you may as well take them.'

'How generous!' exclaimed Witch Hazel. 'They are perfectly frightful, aren't they? We should get a very good price for these.' She stuffed the two spacemen into her shopping trolley, tucked the flying saucer under her arm, and went on her way.

It was not until tea-time that Miss Plint
told Donnabella what she had done with
the garden gnomes.

Donnabella was not in a good mood.
She had spent the whole afternoon trying
to repair the damage to the hemlock
without actually cheating by using magic.

'You did what?' exclaimed Donnabella.

'I sent them to the jumble sale. Even if
you didn't like them, I thought somebody
might want them.'

'Somebody will get quite a shock when it
comes on to rain!'

'Why, what will rain do to them?'
enquired Miss Plint.

'What does rain usually do?' snapped
Donnabella. 'It makes things grow – and I
set the standing-still spell to wear off as

soon as they get back to normal size.'

'You don't mean they're real?' exclaimed Miss Plint. 'Oh, the poor, dear little things! I must save them!' Off she went without even waiting for a second cup of tea.

It took her many weary hours to track them down, glancing up at the sky from time to time to see if it looked like rain.

Witch Hazel remembered the gnomes. She had given them to Greymalkin for the bric-a-brac stall.

Greymalkin said they had definitely been there when she went off to tea, but not when she came back. Try asking the Hag of the Dribble.

At last Miss Plint tracked the two gnomes to a house on the far side of town. They stood guard, one either side of the front door, looking so fierce that Miss Plint was almost too frightened to go up to it and knock.

The door was opened by a small, round, pink-cheeked old lady. 'Good evening,' she said at once. 'So pleased to meet you. I'm Mrs Morgan Jones. You've come about a flat. Eight lovely flats I've got and you can

take your pick. Eight lovely flats. Central
heating. All mod. cons. Just take your pick.'

'Thank you very much,' said Miss Plint,
'but I don't want a flat.'

'No,' said Mrs Morgan Jones, taking out
her handkerchief. 'No one ever does.
Lovely flats they are, too.'

'There, there,' said Miss Plint. 'I'm sure
they are. But I've come about your garden
gnomes. They were sold to you by mistake
and I'd like to buy them back.'

'Oh, no.' Mrs Morgan Jones shook her
head. 'You can't have them. They're my last
hope.'

'You're going to let your flats to garden
gnomes?'

'No-o! What do you think I am? Loopy or
something? I want them to get rid of *him*.
He's driving everyone away.'

'Him?' said Miss Plint.

'The ghost,' said Mrs Morgan Jones.
'Didn't you feel the vibrations when you
came in? Not that I've anything against
ghosts, mind. After all, they've got to go
somewhere, haven't they? Just like anybody
else. But screaming about the place at two
o'clock in the morning! I won't have it.
I said so to Mrs Marchbanks. "You know
what you've got," she said. "You've got bad
vibrations." "But what am I to do about it?"
I said. "Find some good ones," she said.
Then I remembered how my granny always

used to have a couple of gnomes about the place for good luck, and never a ghost or a ghoul or a bump in the night. They'll frighten him off, I thought.'

At that moment there was a shriek from upstairs, followed by a series of thuds, like someone falling downstairs.

'I think he's seen them,' said Mrs Morgan Jones.

'I certainly felt the vibrations,' said Miss Plint. 'Do you think they've frightened him off?'

As if in answer, a low moaning came from outside the door.

'Mrs Marchbanks said it could take weeks,' said Mrs Morgan Jones.

'There may be a quicker way,' said Miss Plint. 'I have a friend who's an expert at magic and – that sort of thing. If she could get rid of the ghost for you, would you let me buy the gnomes back?'

'You can have them as a present. I don't want the ugly things. Come round on Thursday evening.'

If only the weather stays fine till then, thought Miss Plint.

The Confused Ghost
Chapter 6

The weather stayed fine. But Donnabella was being difficult.

'My experience of ghosts,' said Donnabella, 'is don't bother them and they won't bother you.'

'We aren't going to bother it,' said Miss Plint. 'Just have a little chat.'

'I can't find my magic wand.'

Miss Plint glanced towards the vase of flowers on the window ledge, but it was still a vase of flowers, as it had been since she had borrowed it to try out one of Grimalda's *Simple Spells for Simple People*. Spelling was simple enough. It was un-spelling that was difficult. If only she could catch Grimalda for long enough to ask her what she was doing wrong.

'You won't need a magic wand tonight,' said Miss Plint brightly. 'We can look for it in the morning. Mrs Morgan Jones will be waiting.'

So she was. So were a number of other ladies gathered there.

But if Donnabella had been expecting to be the star turn of the evening, that position had already been taken by a large lady draped in shawls and beads.

'Mrs Marchbanks,' said Mrs Morgan Jones respectfully, 'is a medium.'

'Medium what?' asked Donnabella.

'Medium – medium,' whispered Miss Plint. 'She talks to ghosts.'

'Anyone can talk to ghosts,' said Donnabella loudly. 'The point is – does she get an answer?' She looked Mrs Marchbanks straight in the eye. 'I,' said Donnabella, 'am a qualified witch – first class.'

Mrs Marchbanks said nothing. With one hand she gathered her shawls about her, while she rested the other on her forehead and closed her eyes.

'I think she's feeling the vibrations,' whispered Miss Plint.

'Well she won't feel anything over there,' said Donnabella. 'She's miles away.'

The beads jangled angrily as Mrs Marchbanks, pretending not to hear, moved towards the fireplace.

'Cold!' said Donnabella.

Mrs Marchbanks jangled past the fireplace and came to rest by the bookcase. She glared at Donnabella. 'If you don't

mind,' she said icily, 'I am an expert in
these matters.'

'I don't mind at all,' said Donnabella.
'You carry on with your party games, Mrs
Marshmallow, while I go and deal with that
ghost. Shan't be long.' She paused in the
doorway and added, 'Don't give up. You're
getting warmer.'

'I distinctly felt a cold draught then,' said
Miss Plint helpfully, as the door swung to
behind Donnabella.

Mrs Marchbanks sniffed and gave a
disdainful smile. 'Let her go,' she said.
'An unbeliever can be very distressing to
the spirit world. We will begin without her.
Take your seats round the table, and take
the hand of the person on either side of you
– and please remain absolutely silent.'

Miss Plint took her place with the rest. Donnabella seemed to be having all the fun. She could hear her footsteps tramping about the house and Donnabella's voice calling out, 'Hey! Anyone at home?' Then, as she pursued her search upstairs, they were left in complete silence.

Donnabella was really enjoying herself. It was like a game of hide-and-seek. There was definitely a ghost here somewhere – no, he was further up still – yes, it was definitely a 'he' – further up still – finally there was only the attic left, and it was here she finally came upon the ghost, quietly resting. She crept up behind him, then, pulling a simply horrible face, she leapt out, shouting 'Gotcha!' at the top of her voice.

'Aaargh!' screamed the ghost. 'A human!' It leapt on to a chair and stood quivering with fright, while Donnabella calmly looked it up and down.

HAROLD I
HAROLD II
THE RETURN OF HAROLD

'Don't come any closer,' it quavered.
'I'm warning you, I can do terrible things.'
It took a step backwards, fell off the chair
and into a heap on the floor.

'That was pretty terrible,' agreed
Donnabella.

'You tripped me!' said the ghost.

'I did not! I was nowhere near you!'

'I've heard about people like you,'
moaned the ghost. 'Ghost hunters!
Creeping about, setting up traps and tripwires and hidden cameras when a chap's
back is turned, then you trick him into

showing himself so you can show off the pictures to your friends – and then they all come round with cameras and tripwires, and all I can say is . . .' A thought struck him. 'I say, if there is a hidden camera, you will make sure it catches my good side, won't you?' He turned his head round through 180 degrees and gave a sickly grin.

'Now that,' said Donnabella, 'that really does look frightening.'

'If you've just come here to insult me,' said the ghost, 'I think we can consider this conversation at an end.' He stalked out of the room.

He didn't go far. Donnabella found him just outside, his head and one arm sticking out of the opposite wall.

'I appear to be stuck,' he said. 'Would you mind?'

'Ghosts are supposed to be able to walk through walls,' said Donnabella, grabbing the arm and bracing her foot against the wall.

'I can, when I want to,' said the ghost. 'But when there's a perfectly good door, I think it's undignified.'

51

'It is, the way you do it,' said Donnabella, yanking him free. 'But there isn't a door there, anyway.'

'There always used to be,' complained the ghost. 'There used to be a lot of things before all the renovations.' He gave a big sniff of self-pity, and looked ready to dissolve into tears.

'Oh, do pull yourself together,' snapped Donnabella.

The ghost pulled at the shreds of ectoplasm which had begun to drift away. 'I'm sorry,' he said. 'But my nerves are in such a state, I don't know whether I'm coming or going. How would you feel if you couldn't find your way round your own house any more?'

'It isn't your house,' Donnabella pointed out. 'It belongs to Mrs Morgan Jones.'

'I've been here longer than she has,' declared the ghost stoutly. 'A hundred and twenty years, man and ghost. I've never been any trouble. It's not in my nature. But wouldn't you scream if you found yourself stuck inside the central heating at two in the morning?'

Donnabella had to agree she probably would.

'It took me three days to find my way out. And another thing,' he went on, really getting into his stride now. 'No, better still, I'll show you.'

He led the way downstairs – not without two wrong turns, and an embarrassing five minutes in the bathroom.

Signposts for the Ghost
Chapter 7

Outside the sitting-room they could hear Mrs Marchbanks repeating for the umpteenth time: 'Is there anybody there? One rap for yes. Two raps for no.'

The ghost grinned at Donnabella and gave two firm raps on the wall.

There was a ripple of excitement from the ladies in the room.

'No?' exclaimed Mrs Marchbanks. 'Oh, he's a mischievous little fellow, this one. I shouldn't be surprised if he turned out to be a poltergeist.'

'Who's she calling a poltergeist?' demanded the ghost.

Donnabella caught hold of his arm just in time. 'That's the sort of trick she would try,' she said. 'She nearly had you in there.'

'So she did,' he agreed. 'Thank you.'

Inside the room, Mrs Marchbanks called for silence once more and began again: 'One rap for yes. Two raps for no.'

The ghost raised his fist to tap on the wall again. 'Shall I?' he said.

'I wouldn't,' said Donnabella. 'You'll only encourage her. Let's get on with the conducted tour.'

Conducted tour wasn't really the word for it. Mystery tour was more like it. Donnabella, who had been top of the class in Follow-My-Leader at Lady Macbeth's Academy for Young Witches, thoroughly enjoyed herself. Up stairs they went that were no longer there; gliding several centimetres above floors that had been lowered; walking ankle-deep where the floor had been raised (it felt rather like wading through treacle). Donnabella gave up at last when the ghost led her out of a

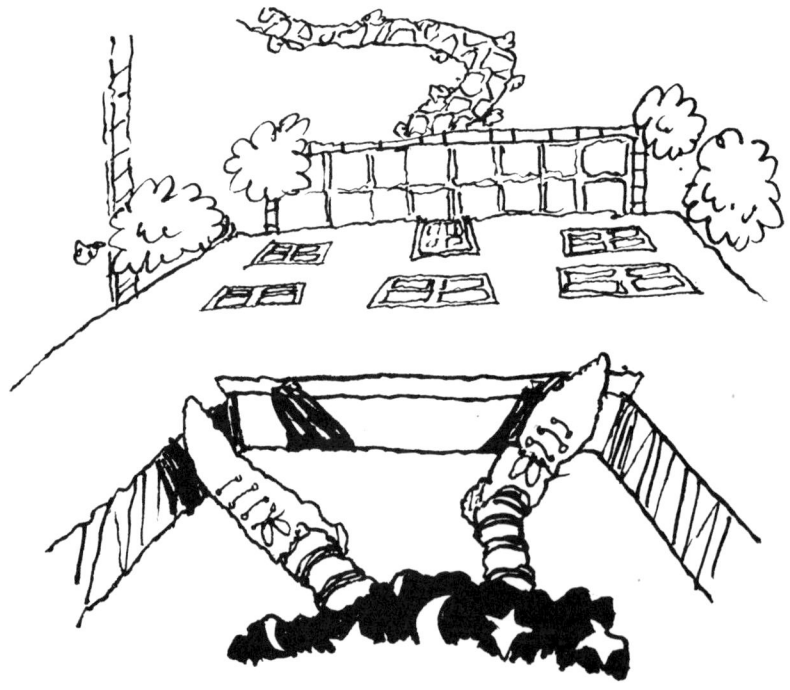

second-floor window and she saw a sheer drop to the ground below. 'This used to be part of the old stable block,' he explained. 'There used to be a connecting door.'

'All right,' said Donnabella. 'You've made your point. You remember the house as it used to be, and you're never going to get used to anything else.'

'But what can you do about it?' sighed the ghost.

'That's easy,' said Donnabella. 'Do you happen to have paper and a pencil handy?'

Some time later Donnabella stuck her head round the sitting-room door:

'Still at it, Mrs Marzipan?'

Mrs Marchbanks was indeed still at it. So far she had tried table rapping and table turning; gone into a trance and come out of it again; tried a little automatic writing; consulted her crystal ball; and all the time felt her audience growing more and more restless. It was almost a relief to see Donnabella's smiling face.

'I should give up,' said Donnabella. 'I think I've solved the problem. Come and see.'

Mrs Marchbanks gathered up her shawls
and sailed out into the hall. She was
brought up short by a notice in
Donnabella's handwriting pinned to the
opposite wall: NO RIGHT TURN.

Mrs Marchbanks turned left and found
another notice: TURN LEFT FOR DINING-
ROOM and in smaller letters: Leading to
Kitchen and Scullery.

The ladies followed the notices round the
house: CAUTION: FIVE METRE DROP;
MIND YOUR HEAD; NO ENTRY; CENTRAL
HEATING. From the attic to the cellar,
every possible hazard was signposted.

Later on, Mrs Morgan Jones took them down and replaced them with neater ones, worked in cross-stitch.

When her lodgers remark on them (eight lovely flats, she has – and all of them always filled), Mrs Morgan Jones smiles and says, 'Oh those! They're for the ghost. So he doesn't get lost. It makes him so nervous, you see.' Which the lodgers find a little strange. Ghost? What ghost? None of them has seen or heard a hint of a ghost in all the time they've been there.

Of course, Mrs Morgan Jones didn't need the garden gnomes any more. 'Take them and welcome,' she said to Miss Plint. 'I think they're frightful. Still, every one to his taste, I suppose.'

Miss Plint thanked her, tucked the spacemen under one arm and the flying saucer under the other, and hurried home. While she was standing in the garden with them, wondering what to do next, she heard a voice call 'Coo-ee!'

Grimalda popped her head over the wall. 'How's the magic going, dear? I've brought another book for you.' She handed Miss Plint a copy of *A Spelling Dictionary for Beginners*. 'Remember,' said Grimalda, 'not a word to Donnabella!' And she was off again before Miss Plint could ask her about turning things back.

She opened the dictionary. Under the letter R she found Rainmaking. Simple: she would make it rain until the gnomes were back to normal. Then she would look under S for Sun and make the weather turn fine again.

She carried everything down to the bottom of the garden, where Donnabella couldn't see her from the house, and set to work. In no time at all a cloud began to form above Miss Plint's head and rain began to fall and the two spacemen and

their ship returned to normal size.

Stiff and dripping wet, Lieutenant Kchw turned to his Captain. 'Will you do the "People of Earth" speech now?' he asked. 'This one seems quite friendly.'

'People of Earth nothing,' snarled Captain Pfft. 'This place isn't safe for us superior beings! I am going to make sure no one else lands here for the next five thousand years!'

'Then may I suggest Emergency Plan C, sir!'

'You may indeed,' said the Captain. 'I'll race you back to the ship.'

Miss Plint watched them go, and waved till the ship was out of sight. Then she turned back to her spellers' dictionary. But under S she found only Snow and Storms. She looked under F for Fine Weather, but it only said Frost. She looked under W for Warm Weather, but it only said Wind. In the end, she just had to leave the cloud still raining at the bottom of the garden, and hope that eventually it would run dry.

She wondered what she would do if it followed her indoors. But it seemed quite content to stay where it was, at the bottom of the garden. She could see it from her bedroom window when she went to bed, and again when she got up in the morning. The rest of the garden was quite sunny, but there was the cloud, raining away.

'Oh, well,' said Miss Plint. 'I expect the frogs like it. I shall just have to work harder so I can get on to Book Three.'

Book Three was a very short book called *Come Fly With Me*. Miss Plint set to work on it in the hope that it would give her some tips on how to control her broomstick.

A Witch for Hallowe'en
Chapter 8

Bump, bump, bump!

Donnabella sat up in bed and listened. There it was again.

Bumpity-bump.

The sound seemed to be coming from downstairs.

Bump, BUMP! Di-di-bump!

Donnabella climbed out of bed and set off downstairs, wishing she had her magic wand for protection.

Slowly she opened the kitchen door, and – 'What on earth do you think you're doing?' demanded Donnabella.

Miss Plint floated towards her, her head bumping gently against the ceiling. 'Getting up here was easy,' she said. 'The difficult bit is getting down. Can you help me?'

'Not until you tell me why you woke me up by banging your head on my bedroom floor.'

'I'm going to be a witch.'

'You what?' screamed Donnabella, so loudly that Miss Plint forgot what she was doing and fell head-first into the log basket.

'Grimalda said you wouldn't like it.'

'Grimalda!'

'She said I have a natural talent. I shall be a witch by Hallowe'en.'

'That mischief-maker! That snake in the grass! That –'

'She's been lending me books.'

'So that's why she keeps dropping in! Borrowing a cup of bats' blood! Collecting for the Home for Unemployed Elves! Asking for my recipe for fairy cakes! Let me see those books!'

'I'm all right at doing spells,' said Miss Plint. 'But undoing them . . .'

'I'm not surprised,' said Donnabella. 'Not one of these spells is complete. 'To Give a Gardener Green Fingers' – all here, except for saying that the dose is a teaspoonful, not the whole bottle.'

'Oh dear,' said Miss Plint. 'Is that why he turned into a geranium?'

'A fine pair of idiots we'd have looked,' said Donnabella, 'if you'd started showing off this stuff at the Hallowe'en revels. They'd have thought I taught it to you!'

'And I wanted to be a credit to you,' sighed Miss Plint.

'And so you shall,' declared Donnabella,

rolling up the sleeves of her nightie. 'We'll
show Grimalda! Where did you get to?
Right! Up you go! And down. And up!
And down. Bend your knees! Chin up!
That's the way!' Once she got down to it,
Donnabella was a merciless teacher.

In a very short time Miss Plint was able
to put right the mistakes she had made.
The wand stopped being a vase of flowers.
The rain stopped over the pond. The
gardener was his old self, none the worse
for having been a geranium for three

weeks – he said he had quite enjoyed it. The young lady in the library, who had mentioned to Miss Plint one day that she wished she could sing like a lark, was very relieved when she stopped making bird-noises every time she opened her mouth.

Miss Plint had high hopes that she would be allowed to join the Coven at the Hallowe'en revels. (Dress formal: wands will be worn.)

'I've got you a present,' said Donnabella. She handed Miss Plint a supermarket carrier bag, which seemed to be empty.

Miss Plint was going to say, A bag for putting things in! How nice! when she felt down the bottom and pulled out a slim, new magic wand.

'You mustn't use it till you're a member of the Coven,' said Donnabella. 'That's against the rules. Now, come on! Let's show Grimalda!'

Miss Plint punched another dent in her brand new hat and nodded.

'Right!' said Donnabella. 'Off we go!'

Up into the October air they soared, first Donnabella, looping the loop, while Miss Plint limped along behind. Broomstick riding was still here worst subject.

She held on tightly with both hands, wishing that broomsticks didn't roll over when you were least expecting it. She was just thinking she was doing better than usual, when the stick gave a jerk and plummeted to the ground. Picking herself up, Miss Plint saw the broomstick leaning jauntily against a lamp-post.

'All right,' she said. 'You can stay there. I'll walk.' The trouble was, which way to go? Everything looked different from down here.

She knocked on the door of the nearest house, but before she could say, Excuse me, could you direct me to Hemlock Hill? she was whisked inside by the young woman who opened the door.

'Thank goodness you've arrived at last! We've been waiting for ages! I must say, I do like your outfit. You really do look like a real witch.'

'Aren't I supposed to?' asked Miss Plint, wondering whether the meeting had been moved indoors and she had come to the right place after all.

The young woman flung open a door and Miss Plint found herself surrounded, not by Donnabella and Grimalda and the rest of the Coven, but a collection of mothers and children.

'OK. Settle down, kids! Our conjuror's arrived, but she can't start till you're all sitting quietly. Mums as well! They're all yours,' she said to Miss Plint. 'Watch out for that little pest Claud – front row, third from the left – he's the sort that never gets invited anywhere more than once.'

Miss Plint found herself facing an

audience who were clearly expecting some
kind of entertainment. Well, why not?
It would be very good practice. She took
a deep breath and began.

The children watched with cries of
delight as out of an old top-hat she
produced two singing birds, and turned a
single handkerchief into a string of flags
which festooned itself round the room.
The waste-paper basket she filled with
sweets, and when everyone had taken all
they could hold, it was still as full as
before. Only one person was not
impressed. That was Claud.

Claud was the sort of person who gets his fun out of spoiling other people's. Whatever Miss Plint produced he said came from up her sleeve. When she made the pumpkin head on the table talk, he said he could see her lips move. When she made it rise in the air and float round the room, he said it was done with strings. All of this was quite untrue. Miss Plint was managing perfectly well without any tricks. If the Coven could have seen her, they would have made her a witch – first class – on the spot. At last Miss Plint leaned forward and hissed, 'If you don't behave yourself, I shall turn you into a frog.'

Claud looked her straight in the eye and said, 'I'd like to see you try!'

Miss Plint should not have done what she did next, but her brand new magic wand was there, and the temptation was just too great. But wands are difficult things to manage, and what she got was not a frog, but a bright green rabbit.

Everyone laughed and clapped, except Claud's mother, who fainted.

The rabbit looked round with a puzzled

expression, until someone felt sorry for it and said, 'All right. Now change him back.'

Miss Plint felt with a sinking feeling the return of her old trouble. She didn't know how. She tried her best, while Claud's mother came round, saw he was still a rabbit, and started to scream.

At that moment Donnabella walked in the door, and a green streak flashed past her and out into the night.

'Oh, stop him!' cried Miss Plint. Too late! 'I turned him into a rabbit,' she confessed. 'Now he won't turn back.'

'You used the wand, didn't you? said Donnabella.

'Yes,' said Miss Plint. 'I'm sorry.'

'You will be,' said Donnabella. 'Claud's mother must have someone to take home. It looks as if it will have to be you.'

Before she could protest, Miss Plint felt herself shrinking. In a few moments she was standing, trying to cover her knees with Claud's grey flannel shorts, while the other children clustered round laughing and Claud's mother flung her arms round her exclaiming, 'Oh, my baby! My baby boy!'

The Green Rabbit
Chapter 9

C laud, meanwhile, after the first rush of excitement, was beginning to feel peckish. He wandered along to the corner shop and looked in the window, but he didn't fancy sweets or crisps. A nice juicy carrot, on the other hand . . .

At that moment Miss Plint came round the corner with Claud's mother clutching her hand.

'It's him!' cried Miss Plint. She wriggled free and set off in hot pursuit, while Claud's mother collapsed in the shop doorway, hoping someone would bring her a nice cup of tea to revive her.

Round the corner, down an alleyway and across the street Miss Plint ran after the green rabbit, out on to the Blasted Heath – and there she lost him.

She sat down on a tree-stump to get her breath back. It was some time before she noticed a rabbit sitting quietly beside her. Even in the moonlight, she could see it wasn't green.

'Oh, bother!' she said.

'Pardon?' said the rabbit.

'I was looking for a green rabbit.'

'A green rabbit,' said the rabbit, 'to my way of thinking, would be something of a rarity. In fact, I don't think I've ever seen one. Rabbits aren't supposed to be green, you know.'

'They're not supposed to talk either,' said Miss Plint.

'And small boys,' retorted the rabbit, 'aren't supposed to be out alone at this time of night.'

'I'm not a small boy,' sobbed Miss Plint. 'I'm a trainee witch. I turned a small boy into a rabbit and if I can't find him I shall have to stay like this.'

'There, there!' said the rabbit. He gave a little chuckle. 'A green rabbit! He shouldn't be hard to find. I'll put out a general call.' He got up and began to beat on the ground with his foot. Then he lay down, put his ear

to the ground and listened. 'Terrible line, this', he said. 'We get a lot of interference from traffic on the motorway.'

He drummed again.

Listened again.

Then he stood up. 'I think he's been seen down by the allotments. Fond of carrots, is he?'

'I don't know. We only met this evening.'

'That's Big Arthur's patch,' said the rabbit. 'Strangers don't last long down there.'

'They won't hurt him?'

'No, no. Just escort him off the premises. He's all right really, is Big Arthur.'

Soon a procession appeared from the direction of the allotments. First came a very big rabbit, with a scar down one cheek and a cauliflower ear – 'Big Arthur,' whispered the rabbit.

After him came at least fifty more, marching in ranks of four, and in the middle, dirty, bedraggled and very

frightened, Claud. He leapt into Miss Plint's
arms, and, thanking them all, she hurried
off to find Donnabella.

Donnabella had had a very annoying
evening, asking everyone she met if they
had seen a green rabbit, and getting
nothing in return but a lot of silly jokes
about pink elephants.

'Please turn him back,' begged Miss Plint.

'I can't do that. It's your spell.'

'I don't know how.'

'Yes you do. Don't you know your fairy
tales? You kiss him.'

'Ugh!' said Miss Plint. 'Must I?'

'Unless you want to stay as you are.
Hurry up. Claud's mother is just round the
corner.'

Miss Plint shut her eyes tight and kissed
the green rabbit. In a moment she was
back to normal and staring down at Claud,
who took one look at these two strange old
ladies and fled. He ran straight round the

corner, right into his mother's arms.

Claud's mother hugged him tight, sobbing, 'My baby! Where have you been? Tell Mummy, darling. Mummy won't be cross.'

'Touching, isn't it?' said Donnabella. 'Come on, there's still time to get to Hemlock Hill.'

'Do you mind if we don't?' said Miss Plint. 'I think I've had enough magic for one night.'

'Don't you want to show Grimalda what you can do?'

'Not really,' said Miss Plint, yawning. 'I know what I can do. You know what I can do. I don't think Grimalda really matters, do you?'

'I suppose not,' said Donnabella. After all, she thought, there was always next Hallowe'en.